A Heart JUST LIKE MY Mother's

For Ada, who has her own kind heart
and her mother's love, always—L.N.

KAR-BEN PUBLISHING, INC.
A division of Lerner Publishing Group, Inc.
241 First Avenue North
Minneapolis, MN 55401 USA
1-800-4-KARBEN
Website address: www.karben.com

Main body text set in Calisto MT Std 18/22.
Typeface provided by Monotype Typography.

Library of Congress Cataloging-in-Publication Data

The Cataloging-in-Publication Data for *A Heart Just Like My Mother's* is on file at the Library
of Congress.
ISBN 978-1-5124-2098-2 (lib. bdg.)
ISBN 978-1-5124-2099-9 (pbk.)
ISBN 978-1-5124-9842-4 (eb pdf)

LC record available at https://lccn.loc.gov/2016059658

Manufactured in the United States of America
1-41266-23238-5/18/2017

by **Lela Nargi**

illustrations by **Valeria Cis**

A Heart
JUST LIKE MY
Mother's

KAR-BEN
PUBLISHING

There are lots of special occasions at Anna's house.

"Rosh Hashanah starts tomorrow," her mother will announce.

Or, "It's the last day of school."

Or, "Your cousin Lucy's turning three!"

On occasions like these, Anna and her mother head
to the crowded subway. They hop a train downtown
to Mr. Reuben's shop.

A visit to Mr. Reuben's is its own special occasion—like a family reunion and a birthday rolled into one.

Inside, the counter twinkles with delicious things to eat: pickles and salads, bagels and lox, and all kinds of nuts and candy.

Mr. Reuben's daughter, Zoe, hands Anna a slice of babka to nibble.

And everyone else who works there cheers, "Hurray, you've come back to see us!" It's as happy and noisy as a parade.

"Your mother is so creative," Zoe tells Anna. "When she was pregnant with you, she bought smoked salmon every week. But she didn't just eat it on bagels. She scrambled it with eggs, she tossed it over salad, she even made it into paté!"

Yum, thinks Anna. But she also thinks, *I could never dream up recipes like that. I'm not creative like my mother is.*

Mr. Reuben remembers when Anna's mother was a girl.

"She always knew how to make us smile," he says. "When she was little, she wore pants on her head, for a hat." He has a fading photograph to prove it.

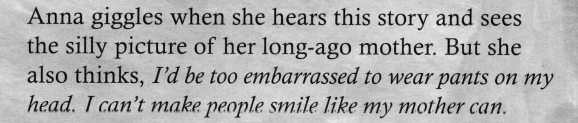

Anna giggles when she hears this story and sees the silly picture of her long-ago mother. But she also thinks, *I'd be too embarrassed to wear pants on my head. I can't make people smile like my mother can.*

At the end of summer, Anna gets sick. She lies in bed and watches the world turn to autumn outside her window. Her mother makes her soup and reads her stories.

When Anna feels better, her mother says, "This is a special occasion! Let's go to Mr. Reuben's to celebrate."

This time when they leave the subway, they see a man sitting on a crate on the sidewalk. He shakes coins in a cup at the fast-moving people rushing past him.

Her mother explains, "He's asking for money to buy something to eat, because he's hungry."

Anna sees her mother tuck two quarters into the cup.

Inside the shop, old Mr. Reuben says, "What'll you have, ladies? Cream cheese? Rugelach?"

Anna has no answer. Her thoughts are drifting out the door and down the block.

The whole way home Anna wonders about the hungry man. Where does he sleep? Does he have a family?

Anna wonders about him as she rides the elevator to her floor.

And as she colors with Sasha from next door.

She wonders about him all through dinner.

She sleeps. She dreams.

When she wakes, Anna
has an idea.

In the recycling bin, Anna finds
an empty shoebox.

She paints it. Then she glues on pictures of bananas and apples and roasted chickens she cuts out of magazines.

She asks her mother to cut a thin slit in the lid.

When Anna gets her allowance, she drops it through the slit in the box.

When she loses her first tooth, she drops the shiny dollar from the tooth fairy into its shadowy depths.

Her birthday comes—and with it, gifts of money from aunts and uncles and grandparents. Into the box it all goes.

Little by little the box grows heavy, until Anna can hardly lift it off her dresser.

Finally, just before Hanukkah, Anna's mother says, "It looks like snow. We'll need emergency provisions from Mr. Reuben's!"

It's the moment Anna has been waiting for.

Tingling with excitement, she struggles to carry her box. Will the hungry man still be there?

Anna and her mother step out of the subway and into winter.

The hungry man is shivering on his crate on the sidewalk.

Inside the shop comes the usual cry: "You're here at last! What'll it be? Whitefish? Potato salad?"

Anna lifts the box to the counter.

"I want to buy bagels for the man on the crate, for whenever he's hungry," she says. "Is this enough money?"

She lifts the lid. A treasure load of coins and bills winks in the box.

For a long moment, the shop is silent. Then Mr. Reuben steps out from behind the counter.

"When your mother was a girl," says Mr. Ruben, "she used to buy bagels, too, to bring to a homeless shelter down the block." Then he reaches into the box and lifts out three shiny coins. "This will be enough for the first bagel," he says.

Outside, Mr. Reuben puts
a bagel in the man's hand.

Anna watches as the man's
surprised face breaks into a smile.

Zoe bends down to Anna's height.

"You have a big heart," she says.

And Anna knows that this is what makes her just like her mother.

About Tzedakah

In this story, Anna performs an act of tzedakah—she gives to someone in need. The highest form of tzedakah is to give without any expectation of recognition or thanks. The man with the cup will not know that Anna provided the money for his bagels. Some people translate the Hebrew word "tzedakah" as "charity," but the word really means "righteousness." We are doing the right thing when we help others.

About the Author

LELA NARGI wrote her first story in a notebook with a marbled cover her mother bought her the summer before she started first grade; she's been writing ever since. She lives in Brooklyn, New York, with her husband and daughter, and a very large rabbit.

About the Illustrator

VALERIA CIS was born and raised in Argentina, where she still lives with her son, Facundo, daughter, Olivia, and husband, Sebastian. Valeria studied fine art at the University of Humanities and Arts in Rosario, Argentina.